A RAPPER'$
QUEEN

A NOVEL

mmandi

QUART-DE-LUNE

MMANDI

A Rapper'$ Queen

ISBN 978-2-9810534-8-0

Legal Deposit : Bibliothèque et Archives nationales du Québec, 2015

Legal Deposit : Library and Archives Canada, 2015

*If you've got it,
Flaunt it!*

****

1

So here it is. I am sitting there, trying to catch my breath, thinking: « What now? ». Now that I've made it well, now that I've got much more than I'll ever need for the rest of my life, what's next?

Much more than I need, indeed: a lavish house in Florida, a magnificent loft in Manhattan, a villa in the South of France, an apartment in Barra, too many expensive vehicles, a beautiful yacht, sumptuous couturier dresses, designer shoes and bags and accessories that I have ceased to count, pricey jewels which have been insured with serious insurance companies.

And the money! Most of all, the money! Money. Lots of it!

What else? So much more I can't think of. Beside the things, the blings and many hundred millions of dollars, not to forget the grand lifestyle.

And what else? We also had our own airplane. We? Well, my husband and I. My husband, the man I passionately loved, the man I was crazy about. That's right: my husband and I, rich couple in a little world. That's it: a little world! Because once you've reached that level of money, you are given fast and easy access to everything you need or desire. And then the world suddenly appears small. No boundaries, no borders anymore; you always find yourself where you want to be, whenever it pleases you. And all is just right there for you, whenever it pleases you. Yeah. That's what we call "living the life".

2

I grew up in New Jersey. My parents had bought a house in Teaneck. A little house that I used to find beautiful, with two bedrooms, a kitchen and a living room into which was squeezed a dinner area. This part of the house was only utilized when we had special guests. The rest of the time, the chairs, the armchairs and the couch were covered with grayish old bed-sheets in order to keep the furniture fresh.

Since the 9-11 tragedy, my father felt the urge to proclaim his love for our country. Hence, outside our house, right over the front door, a magnificent United States flag was flapping in the wind. And, believe me, that was a beautiful sight.

We were very proud to have our own home and content that our kitchen table never lacked the daily food. My sister Arlene and I shared the smaller sleeping room and my parents had a king size bed in theirs. Thus we really felt we were rich because everything in the little house was big. So much so, the tall dresser would seem glued to the left side of the dinner table overhanging six fat yellow armchairs, which gave the impression they were all stuck to each other. I remember one day my girlfriend Takisha, for whatever reason, happened to enter my parents bedroom.

— Men, these are some expensive stuff! she said.

In fact, the king size bed was so massive there was no place to walk around. Yeah, these were indeed expensive stuff!

We particularly felt rich, one specific summer, because my dad had bought a brand-new car. It was a shiny white sedan that no other vehicle in the neighborhood could compare to. And I started to believe that we were on top of the world; that we were the best of the best. Everybody would look at us going along through the New Jersey's streets. I guess they were looking at us out of admiration, well, perhaps with a bit of envy. But anyway, it was a good feeling. And, on Sundays, when we would go to church, we'd often wear some fine-looking outfits and a touch of perfume. I would then hold my head up high, certain that nothing in the world could ever bring us down.

However, facing our house, there was a young man everyone called Stex. I never knew where that nickname came from. The thing is: Stex was good-looking in every way you could ever imagine. He was blond, he was tall, he was everlastingly tanned. He was handsome and he was handsome and he was handsome. And he was, more than anyone else, fascinated with his own self. The feminine tribe, of course, was constantly twirling around him. But somehow that guy was my very first infatuation. Yeah, I was in love with Stex. Unrequited love that is. I guess many of us were learning, at the same time, what it was to love and not getting love back. As for myself, I didn't have a little chance: too many beautiful candidates for a single guy! One of them named Tracy seemed to be his favorite; so I sort of hated her. She was a tight

11

dress short skirt lots of makeup kind of girl and I especially despised her trashy style.

Nevertheless, I was considering Stex as a potential boyfriend, one I could finally win if I was good enough, patient enough, nice enough. But, as time went by, I realized that was obviously not going to happen. Still I kept on hoping and fantasizing about him. And I would probably do something desperate in the end, in order to catch Stex's affection. Happily, my sister and I had a strong father keeping his eyes on us.

My father had come from somewhere in the Connecticut and had made his way to find himself at a nice position in a great shoe company. He had started there as a low paid operator, had worked hard for many years and had finally become a respected foreman. But, in spite of his status there, he kept working long hours, starting very early in the morning until quite late in the evening. My mother used to tell him:

— Henry, you have to slowdown. These long hours at the factory are killing you.

— Well, Barb, a man gotta do what he gotta do, he would answer.

My mother is of Greek descent but considers herself a pure American. Her grand-parents had immigrated in the United States where they had given birth to my mother's mother and three other children. Every now and then, all of her relatives would gather for some celebration and you would realize how large a family they are.

Now you have to understand that even though I look white, I am not. My mother's mother had married an Afro-American; so my mother, my sister and I are in fact black.

My mother was more a peach carnation colored woman with kinky hair. My sister and I were fair-skinned with dark brown curly hair and green eyes. Since we were little, my mother had used all kind of techniques to sleek our hair so we could easily blend in. I guess she thought she would please her mother's family by doing that. Nonetheless, this condition of ours was responsible for an identity confusion, as we felt white in Afro-Americans' gatherings and we felt black when we were among white people.

My grandmother's marriage with a black man had caused lots of turmoil within her folks. For many years, she'd stayed apart from her parents and siblings. However, as time went by, they all finally came to their senses. And once again, they were a big united cluster.

But the one Arlene and I loved the most was my mother's mother. Our grandmother was a kind and fine-looking woman. She had probably spoiled us too much; at least that's what my father used to say. She would often give us pocket money, she would buy us all kinds of gifts and goodies. Her home had always been joyful, a place where everyone was greeted with mouth-watering cooking and thrilling music, though all that had changed when her beloved husband died.

My father was the backbone of our family. He would provide for us all. My mother was a good housewife but had no significant employment skills. Her priority was to raise us well, my sister and me. She kept the place all clean and beautiful, cooked and baked, helped us with our homework. My mother would go from job to job, happy to bring the extra cash. She would work as a mill hand in a factory, as a vendor in a store or even as a waitress in a restaurant. Later, she would find herself working as a care giver in an elderly citizens' residence.

Both my mom and dad were honest folks, and pretty religious too. They were a little bit conservative and wished to see us walking in their paths, adopting the same old traditions they had followed all their life. And somehow they had succeeded at transmitting to us good values. I do believe that all those guidelines we'd received during childhood are still with us, in our mind, in our heart or maybe somewhere else. But I am sure they remain in us, sometimes hidden and sometimes crystal clear.

Our parents were very proud of us. We were well-mannered, respectful and we loved them dearly.

Arlene was more intelligent than any girl I knew. Everybody would shake their head and pay a compliment: « Henry, what a smart young lady you have there! » or « I foresee such a bright future for this child, Barbara! ». But about me, all they would say is: « Jenny is such a sweet girl! ».

Nevertheless, I used to consider I was a great success. My grades at school have always been good enough. Besides, I had taken classical dance lessons for many years. My sister had preferred music, and so she has learned classical piano. With my mother, everything had to be classical. This state of mind must have been a result of her Greek background. She used to say that the Greeks are highly inclined to everything grandiose. In the end, my sister would switch from classical to jazz and I had quit ballet for modern dances.

My sister Arlene is three years older than I am, but we understood each other well. She cared a lot for me and I was aware of that. Arlene was a wise young girl; I'd always confided my stories to her and asked her for advice. And when I met Gregory, my first love, she told me:
— Jenny you're only 14 years old, you don't have to rush anything.

16

— I am not rushing anything; I truly love him, I answered.

— Anyway, sis, just take it slow!

I was 16 when I began to work at the shoe factory during my vacations. Arlene had already done so for many times and she had a good employment resume. As for myself, I first found it sad and difficult to waste my free times, especially in the summer. But soon enough, it felt great having my own money; and working had then become the prelude of recurrent rewards. I had saved most of my cash but didn't deprive myself of squandering the rest of it in all kind of fancy expenses.

At 20 years old, Arlene started a full time job as a manager's assistant in a sizable cosmetic company. She had finished college with flying colors and it was certain that she'd soon be climbing up the career ladder. From her first paycheck, my sister had contributed substantial amounts for the monthly family's expenses; and things went better and better at home.

One early morning, while sleeping, I was startled by a scream coming from my parents' room.

I jumped out of my bed and ran, in order to find out what was that commotion about. I just could not believe my eyes after I crossed their door. There was my father, laying on the floor, near the king size bed.

— Call the ambulance! Call the ambulance! was yelling my mother.

However Arlene was already on the phone; the ambulance was to arrive soon. Alas, nothing could be done to save my dad. It was a massive heart attack and he died on his way to the hospital.

After my father departed, life was not the same. We were always sad. My mother fell into a long and severe depression, so she could barely work. Financially, things started to deteriorate. Then within a few months, it all went wrong. Arlene's contribution was far from sufficient to keep the house going. Rapidly, we became poor. I'd continued to go to college but was no more disposed to study. My grades kept going downward and I was mortified. I used to be such a proud girl, now the students were laughing. And behind my back, they were calling me « Jenny penny ». I was so humiliated.

It was Autumn. The leaves were falling from the trees and the flowers had died. The yellowish gardens I formerly enjoyed seemed to mirror my bruised spirit. It would have taken a great deal of courage for me to continue on the same path. Instead of holding on, I decided to give up school. I stayed home a few days, brooding on the disaster my life had become. After that, I went out looking for work. Two weeks later, I had found myself a job as a general clerk in a Community Center.

It didn't take long for Gregory to let me down. He was a very handsome black fellow; it would be so easy for him to replace me. To this young man I had called my boyfriend, I was currently a girl with no prestige, no future. He had, over the years, possessed my body and my soul, but he had promised me he would always be there for me. Now I wasn't interesting anymore; he no further desired any part of what I had turned out to be. Hence he announced me coldly that he was leaving me. I was stunned. I just could not believe Gregory was that cruel. I cried, I begged, I sobbingly asked what I had done wrong, and I assured I would do for him anything he wanted.

But my pain and my tears had no effect on him. He left without blinking. And it became obvious to me that I was, like my mom, heading for a huge depression.

3

I don't like recalling this moment of my life. It was indeed my first encounter with despair. I had no ammunition to stand for myself and fight away that overwhelming grief. My mother was in her own distressing world and my sister Arlene was pushing hours between two jobs trying to make ends meet. I was all alone in this.

The following year was filled with days which seemed darker and darker. From time to time, I would regain hope that there was still a possibility for reconciliation with Gregory. And I would telephone him, convinced that he was missing me as I was missing him, but only to hear him shout at me:
— Would you stop that, Jenny! Stop bothering me! Get a life! Leave me alone! You hear me: leave me alone!

I would beg, I would cry, I would supplicate. And he was as usual: merciless. Those were the worst evenings. I would spend the whole night sobbing and would only fall asleep in the early morning. Then after two or three hours, I would get up with that nauseous feeling in my stomach, realizing that nothing good was out there for me. Nonetheless I had to leave my bed, get to work and stay there for eight long hours. By chance, being a general clerk in the Community Center required no specific skills and, during those days, I would just function as an automaton.

My girlfriends Courtney and Takisha visited me often during that period. I guess that's what kept me going.

Courtney was a 5'6'' average girl: long auburn hair, probably too skinny, no especially great feature. She was a T-shirt and jeans no make-up type, as were many classical ballet students in my dance classes. In fact, she would be totally insignificant without her clear blue eyes. She was quiet and soft-spoken; a girl who would always see the positive side of all things.

Takisha was completely different. She was a black bombshell. She would go to parties all the time and she was very popular. I always had the feeling she was strong and fierce. We became friends at the dance school. She was in a modern dance group and she was fantastic. My dad didn't like her much.

— This girl has a bad influence on you, he'd say.

— Is it because she's black? I'd answer.

— Would you stop that nonsense!

My father would then rave for a while. I guess he didn't appreciate my innuendo. There had been racial tension in our vicinity, not too long ago; so my question was indeed very upsetting. He eventually calmed down and, in the end, explained that he was neither a racist nor a xenophobe. He would not have married my mother if he was anything like that. I guess my father just didn't like Takisha because she was too sexy, too adventurous and too open-minded.

The steady presence of my two girlfriends had helped me through that difficult time of my life. I'd probably not have recovered without them. Although it took me many months before I felt better.

Once I'd gotten better, I started noticing many things which I had eluded while I was suffering. First of all, my mother was in a very bad shape. She would seat all day gazing into space, looking vaguely at something that seemed far away. It was obvious her distress was soaring. Arlene, my sister, did not realize the potential danger. She was working so hard; she was exhausted. When she came home at night, she would just eat, watch a little TV and go to bed. Really, I was on the verge of panicking; it was clear something had to be done, and as quick as possible. So, one evening, I decided I would have a chat with mom myself.

— Mam, how are you today? I asked.

— Good. How about you, Jenny?

— I'm okay, mam. But let's not talk about me. Tell me: how you feel today?

— I just told you I'm well.

— But mammy, you don't look well at all.

— What do you mean?

— I mean you don't look well, and you've got to do something.

— But what exactly do you mean?

— That you are very depressed and that you should seek help.

My mother did answer nothing. Perhaps she was too down to sustain a conversation. I insisted and I promised I'd accompany her if she agreed to go through such a process. She only shook her head. Well, I took that as a « Yes ». And one week later, I was taking her to a group therapy session for recent widowers.

What I noticed also was the state of our house. Everything in our home used to be nice and neat. Now dishes were all over the drain board and clothes scattered on the floor. It looked to me as a deserted place, except for that disgusting smell of garbage floating in the air. Frankly, I couldn't see how on earth things would ever be put back the way they were before.

Meanwhile, Takisha was looking more glamorous than ever. She had clearly attained a new scale of sophistication. It was obvious to me that she was wearing very expensive clothes and shoes and accessories. One day, Courtney and I were sitting on the porch chatting when she came to visit. She was all glittering with her heavy gold chains and bracelets. I knew jewels like that were out of our reach; so I was a little bit concerned.

— Hey girl, you look prosperous! You must've found yourself a good job, I told her.

— I guess you could say so.

— Oh, good for you! said Courtney.

— Is it in a great company? I asked.

— Jenny, you know, there's a whole wide world out there.

— What does that mean?

— That I am not the kind of girl to work in a company. I am a dancer and I dance.

— You dance?

— Yep! I dance; this is what I do, right? This is what I love to do. I dance… mostly for hip-hop videos.

— Really? But, does that pay well?

— It does, actually.

— You never told us…

— Yeah, how come you never told us?

— It's funny, I never thought of telling anybody.

— Why? Is it supposed to be a secret?

— Not really. Just I'd never thought that would interest anyone.

— Well, it does interest me.

— And same for me, said Courtney.

— We are dancers too; remember?

— Means what?

Takisha asked that question, but I am sure she already knew the answer. Courtney and I went both to the dance school since we were kids, and we were definitely interested in such a fun job that paid so well.

Actions say so much more than words. You will assess someone's friendship by his or her actions. Takisha was a real friend. She quickly made the connections and, next thing we had known, we were part of a group of young dancers practicing on a song for a coming video shooting.

That's how everything started. We became pop music videos' background dancers. It was quite cool and the money was good enough. It was indeed a lot of fun. It was a whole new life, and Gregory wasn't in it. I had completely stopped thinking of him.

I remember my first weeks as a dancer in the group. Juanita —whose parents came from a South-American country 40 years ago— offered me a fast and easy comradeship. She was a friendly girl and, since I was a new recruit, I was fairly pleased.

As I was telling Juanita the stories of my life; she seemed very empathetic. But when it came to Gregory, she looked at me with a despising expression, as if she was in front of some infectious moron.

— You've gotta be kidding! she said.

— Why's that?

— How could you fall for such a guy?

— I don't know. I was in love with him, I think.

— Lady, you don't even respect yourself! What did that guy offer you?

— Well, he is very handsome…

— Some girls are born stupid. Me, I would never fall for a guy who could not offer me a dime.

— You mean you just love for money?

— But of course, my dear! What else should I love for?

— What if the guy is the right guy for you?

— The right guy for me is a guy who has lots of money.

— Oh yeah?

— Oh yes! Listen, lady, I'm good-looking, I am hot, I got good stuff and I got skills. There is a price for that. And, believe me, the price is high!

— Oh really?

— Yes, really. Stop being stupid, little Jenny!

28

From that day, I never talked about Gregory again. I suppose Juanita's speech had utterly erased him from my mind; it was as if he'd never existed.

Being background dancers was a whole new life for us, exciting but very demanding. We could find ourselves practicing the same moves over many days, and then we'd arrive on a shooting set and be asked to rearrange the whole choreography. Nerve-racking! Often, when we got home after a day of work, we had bruises over our feet and our muscles were aching beyond belief. But, we had learned to deal with those situations. As we were young enough, our body could easily recover from the stress it had to endure.

We were dancing with various types of artists and for various types of events. But working with the rappers was the most challenging. We often had to dance with break dance performers and it was quite difficult to keep up with them. Some of the B-boys and B-girls were stupendous; they would be ready to take risks that ordinary dancers were not willing to take.

Also, we had soon gotten accustomed to expose ourselves. The performing costumes were more and more revealing; that was the way to go in this business. We just had to teach ourselves to be comfortable with nudity, or else. As one of the producers let us know soon enough. He was fuming because Courtney had said she didn't want to show that much of her body. His face turned all red and his eyes looked as those of a mad man, while he shouted at her:

— We need no nuns here! Well, if you feel like one, just get out of my face! Get out now! Get out; find yourself a convent!

That was a traumatic experience. We learned a lesson that day: our body was our bread and butter; we were paid to exploit it as far as we could possibly go. And that was just the beginning.

So Courtney changed her ways. She started wearing very tight clothes, high heels and a lot of make-up. She would be walking now twisting her hips and throwing out her chest, in an attempt to bring out her buttocks. She would even adopt a lower speaking tone, as if she had been a long time smoker. Courtney was becoming so sexy I hardly recognized her.

It finally happened that our group had been called by a huge casting firm. We would have the chance to perform in an outstanding dance movie and the money was going to be great. We were booked for six weeks and we had to travel through the States and abroad.

Traveling was a first for me. We'd be shooting in Toronto, Montreal, New York and then Miami. So here I was, sitting in a plane heading to some location called Canada. I never ever thought that one day I would fly away from my country. To me, the United States of America was the world, that's it and that's all. I never had to question whether another country existed. I must admit though, traveling was terribly exciting.

During all the time shooting, we were located in sumptuous hotels and we were fed fine foods. Let's say we kind of felt like royalty. Personally, I was discovering what luxury was all about. And I sensed right away that the life I had known until then was definitely mediocre. I was also realizing there were other terrific places beyond my own country. I grew up believing that the United States was the sole decent place on earth. Suddenly I was glancing at a larger world, a fabulous world I'd never thought existed. But still, I was glancing from a distant window, wondering if one day I'd be a part of it.

4

My mother was making progress. She looked revitalized. She chatted with us more often and she even smiled from time to time. But then, two years had passed since father's death. One day, when I got home, the supper was ready; she had surprisingly prepared the meal.

Our financial situation had finally improved. Arlene and I were bringing money home, so we could afford more than the bare necessities. Thanks God, my father had completed payments for our house, many years ago.

Takisha was now dating a baseball player. He certainly was a wealthy guy; he was handsome on top of that. Takisha was ecstatic to have gotten his attention. She never told us how she'd met him though. I guess Courtney and me and all the other girls were a little bit envious. Some might have been squarely resentful. The fact is, in this business called show business, the artists are highly competitive. In our group of dancers, most of us were "Material girls". The expensive new bags, the blings or other costly stuff they'd acquired, along the rich men they had planned to conquer, that was all they would keep on talking about. We were definitely in a gold digger's culture.

Among us, we had a little name for those who seemed excessively inclined to search for wealthy mates: we called them G-ggaz, a contraction form for gold diggers. Perhaps nearly all of us thought we were excluded from such a pattern. But in reality, craving for rich lovers was like a contagious disease and we had become in the end all a bunch of G-ggaz.

Well, Juanita was one girl who didn't have a problem with words. As she was telling me about a guy she had just met, she was practically counting in dollars the advantages she had planned to collect from that relationship. I was kind of disturbed by such cynicism. So I said:
— Juanita, you are a freakin G-ggaz!

— But of course, my dear. And I'm very proud to be a freakin G-ggaz.

Yeah, I was learning a lot of stuff with Juanita!

Courtney had left on a trip to Atlanta. She had spent two months there. When she came back, she had a new nose, extra large bosoms and inflated lips. Courtney was now a glamorous reddish hair bimbo. Well, it was quite a shock. And now, to the dismay of all the other girls, every man who saw her became like a frisky dog hankering after a tantalizing bone.

I did not realize I was changing too. Like the other girls, I was now buying sexy designer clothes and high heels. I had changed the color and texture of my hair; I became a platinum blond with shiny silky hair. I had assumed it well-matched my light green irises. But maybe the beholders' eyes had seen something different because, all of a sudden, people in New Jersey would stare at me, shake their head and say:

— Jenny, you are something else!

Believe it or not, I thought they were then paying me a compliment, that they sort of perceived me like a star. But I am now certain they were rather a little bewildered; they did not understand at all what they were looking at and were probably wondering what had happened to me. I guess that's how it is: too often, a lot of people will stop liking you or will ridicule you, whenever you begin to make a few moves toward your way up. Nevertheless, I had felt really great with my new look.

One other thing: the girls in the dance team who had formerly seemed kind to us now started to be mean. They were openly rude and, from time to time, they would throw nasty remarks to Courtney and me. I was wondering why they were acting so wickedly. But until Takisha brought us an explanation, we couldn't figure out what was the reason for that.

— It's just because you look good now.

— No! Seriously?

— This is a very competitive world, you know.

— Are you telling me that they are jealous?

— Well, you can call it whatever you want. But being in any group of performers is like being on a risky hunting ground.

— Meaning?

— Be cautious: anything could happen!

So Courtney and I were looking good and we were sexy too. Thus, now we represented new competition they needed to suppress. That was some sort of sad lesson to learn. I had really thought we were a loyal and friendly team; my ingenuousness was definitely losing ground. I was discovering that this world could be a complicated place.

It was one of those gray mornings that urge you to stay in your bed and sleep late. Happily, I had no specific appointments; so I cozily kept myself under the eiderdown until noon. I was indolently leaving my room, heading to the shower, when the telephone rang. I was in no mood for talking but picked it up anyway. It was Anny, the manager's assistant for the dance group. She explained to me that we had been called to work with JupitA, a very prominent rapper, and that I had to come to the studio as quick as possible.

The contract was about a video shooting for one particular JupitA's song related to a soon to be released album. We would feature as background dancers but would have to work closely with the rapper's posse. I never had the chance to act in the presence of a well-known rapper. For me, that was a big event. I also knew that there would be aggressiveness and mental fights between the girls, in order to win JupitA's attention. Yeah, I could not agree more with Takisha: that was indeed a very competitive world.

Anyway, we had well received that assignment because JupitA didn't have a bad reputation, although he was an overconfident performer. He was not the kind of rapper to disrespect another rapper for the sake of competition. In Hip-hop, those days, any lack of respect could trigger a bloodshed. From what I heard, to those who had insulted him and were awaiting a response, he once replied: « Oh no, I have nothing to say. I ain't gonna diss any damned hater over some stupid words… No, no, this battle is not mine to fight, you know what I'm sayin! »; which led me to suppose that he believed in a higher power. He wasn't interested in feeding conflicts; he just wanted to do his thing, that's it that's all.

The making of the video was much harder than I had anticipated. Of course, we had rehearsed many times at the dance studio. Still, we had to go through many takes for each shot. Our performance had to do with a lot of booty clapping and swaying from the hips. The moves were dangerously abrupt and the cadence was pretty fast too. Let me tell you, it was not easy. So we would spend long hours carrying out the same motions over and over again.

We were all fascinated by JupitA's demeanor. He wasn't particularly handsome, just an average looking black guy. He arrived in a silver gray Bentley Mulsanne, wearing jeans and a leather jacket that was obviously costly. And of course, he accessorized his clothing with heavy gold chains, a few big rings and a diamond grill. « Well, show me your grill! » they say. I remember the first time I'd noticed that metallic device on a rapper's teeth. It was on a TV show. I had really thought it was some orthodontic apparatus. Later, I'd learned that it was rather an expensive jewel! Then, the grill kept evolving in sophistication. And it had become a symbol of status in the Hip-hop world.

Anyway, all of us in the dance group were well aware of the many different symbols adopted by the wealthy artists, according to their types. We were definitely capable to appraise the kinds of money we'd have in front of us. And by looking at JupitA, we knew we were looking at big money.

I've never been the type of girl to fight for a man's attention, even if he was JupitA. It always seemed to me that women would benefit more from making common cause with each other. So I kept my focus on the job, only trying to give it my best shot. Nevertheless, I noticed that JupitA was kinda looking at me during the takes. But then, I thought it was another stupid delusion. Over and over again, we had seen women mistakenly believing important men were interested in them. It was generally because each of those women had the pretention of being the most beautiful girl in the world. They were dreaming their own dream that had nothing to do with the reality. Well, that was the sort of booby-trap I didn't wanna be part of. However, soon enough, I saw JupitA coming toward me. It was a stunning moment. He came and stood in front of me. Then he told me straight out:

— Yo, shawty, you're smoking hot!

— Thank you.

— Listen, gorgeous, we need to have a fuck.

I thought I was going to fall. I was so shocked and insulted! I opened my mouth: « How dare you? » I was about to say. Then, for whatever reason, Juanita's words came to my mind and convinced me to approach the situation in another fashion.

— What did you say? I asked instead.

— I said let's go fuck.

— Oh really? …But then, we need to talk.

— Talk? Talk about what?

— Talk about bucks.

— Yeah? And how much?

— A lot.

— Oh yeah? Why's that?

— Because I got good stuff and I got skills.

He laughed and looked at me, as if he had just noticed me for real. And then he took me by the hand, calmly heading to his bedroom, followed by three other guys that I later learned were his security escorts.

I guess in every girl lays a wild bitch. That bitch could remain forever dormant or, for some reason, it could suddenly wake up. And now, mine was about to burst.

I spent the whole night in his room. And I enjoyed every second of it. In the morning, he handed me something. I knew exactly what it was: yes, a bundle of cash!
— BMF, he murmured.
— What's that?
— Blowing money fast, he explained.
— Well, good for you!

I had spoken softly, even though I took the tone of someone who was accustomed to that kind of treatment. In fact, I was really emotional; I had never before held so much money in my hand. « BMF », he had said! I'd heard the rumor about rich rappers going to discotheques and literally throwing many thousands of dollars in the air. That's how they were blowing their money fast!

But I'd not yet had the chance to experiment the phenomenon.

The shooting for the video was wrapped up that day. I'd imagined seeing JupitA afterward. I was hopeful he would spend a moment with me and that we would keep contact. But he left that same evening; he didn't even take the time to say goodbye. I am still wondering today if he had remembered having sex with me the night before. I guess, to him, I was just one among a multitude of girls, a temporary toy. I was ashamed; it was hard to believe someone could be so cold. Perhaps I had groundless expectations. Perhaps I had naively thought that the sizzling night we had spent together would make him consider me as his real girlfriend. Obviously, that was not the case. And I was crushed.

Later, when I got home, I was all gloomy and down. I just threw my clothes on a chair and my handbag on the floor. I was about to enter the shower when it came to my mind: the cash! And, at that same moment, I knew what had happened. I knew exactly what it was: I might've been perceived by JupitA as some sort of handy sex worker. More precisely, I might have behaved like one. Yeah, it was now clear to me. That's it: I wasn't a girlfriend, I was just a whore! Well, believe me, that was a shock. That was a big shock. Nevertheless, I rushed to the bag and grabbed the money he had given me. And I started to count. I counted: 10 grand! And then, I recounted. Still 10 000$! I'd never seen so much money in my life. Almost half of my sister's annual salary! Except that I've earned it in one night. My sadness swiftly vanished in thin air. And it just felt fantastic. Exhilarating! From that moment, I knew what I really wanted. From that moment, let me tell you, little Jenny-the-sweet was no more.

At this point in my life, I had already been acquainted many times with disappointments and sorrow. There was a valuable lesson to learn from those experiences: pains come and pains go. For whatever reason, you will get up one day and they will disappear. It's only a matter of time. Once you understand that, you're sure to be able to support sufferings with courage and patience, knowing that somehow they will pass.

Considering my former expectations that had led all to disillusionment, I told myself that I had nothing to lose. I was now ready to grasp anything I could get. Only, this time, I was craving after concrete, tangible things. It occurred to me that, as I was pretty, it would probably be much easier. There is always a man somewhere ready to give to a young pretty girl whatever she would ask. All I had to do was to keep my eyes wide open, and spot those men.

Now I was ready to do what I had to do. So I decided I would dress even sexier: my dresses were shorter and my high heels higher. Well, it didn't take more than that. As a performer, I was crossing the paths of rich men who seemed to always need some sweet. And here I was, all prepared to bring what they wanted. Some of them were good-looking, some were not. But they all had a lot of money; so to me, handsome or not handsome, it made no difference. I only thought of the green bucks and everything was fine. I'd sometimes bend my knees, close my eyes, open my mouth and let it blow. Sometimes a quick hand job between two takes during a video shooting would be as satisfactory for the receiver and for me. I'd get the extra cash and he'd get... a release. Often, though, I would lie down or I would just bend down, allowing the worker to work hard at his own pleasure.

For some reason, those moments were always enjoyable to me. Perhaps I was turning into a sex addict. Perhaps the prospect of great cash to come had something to do with my gladness. Or perhaps I got it good both ways: my heart was beating to the sound of money and my body was craving for sex. Yeah, I guess that's how it was. But above all, I just had money on my mind!

5

Hip-hop was flying high. Funny, because in the 1980's everybody was saying hip-hop would not go far. When —thanks to Run-D.M.C.— it had spread out from the States to the other countries, people all over there thought that it was just a onetime success, a trend which would last only one or two or three years. Surprisingly, hip-hop took over the music industry everywhere. The youngsters were instantly captivated by the movement while their parents were outraged, claiming that such kind of music was inciting to rebellion and violence. Nevertheless, hip-hop kept growing stronger and stronger. It was like a storm which kept on storming. And, soon enough, the hip-hoppers became worldwide celebrities; then they got richer and richer and richer.

So we had seen the rise of Dr Dre, P. Diddy, Jay-Z, Snoop Dogg, Kanye West, Fifty Cent, Birdman, LL Cool J, Timbaland, Busta Rhymes, Wyclef Jean and also the Black Eyed Peas with Lady Fergie. I like to call her Lady Fergie, just because she is naturally sexy and that she could be so without the least vulgarity. Then came the first wide-reaching white rappers: Vanella Ice and EMINEM. And last but not least, hip-hop female artists like Missy Elliott, Eve, Queen Latifah and Lil' Kim who were going strong too.

Along the wealth came the rivalry. And from time to time, you'd hear one of the great rappers had been gunned down. That was rather scary. As dancers in the hip-hop world, we were sometimes concerned about our own security. However, we kept on going. As dancers, what else could we have done? Perform only in children festivities or community celebrations? Dancing for hip-hop was difficult but fun and the pay also was good. But, above all, we were meeting interesting people we could have never met in any other circumstances.

I was from time to time in the same video shooting than Juanita. I was then beholding the master seductress in action. She had her way of attracting male's attention. While Courtney had just to be somewhere for all the men to come running, Juanita had developed a few hooking techniques. She would rapidly spot any potential big spender and she'd wait for the right moment to act. She would seem totally indifferent. And then suddenly, she would turn to the targeted one and say something banal while she would simply touch his arm or give him a friendly tap on his back. All of this was rapidly executed and seemed absolutely unintended. However, the connection was made. She would, later on, accidentally find herself in front of that chosen guy and she would smile innocently. Juanita was gifted with that kind of Latina's beauty who'd raise her preys' temperature once she'd got their attention. She had wide black eyes and small well aligned teeth. A childlike smile and a perfectly shaped woman's body: that was definitely a gold-digger's decoy for rich sexual perverts.

Thus, I was learning from the master and I was playing my own game. A few men had taken me out. It was always an opportunity for me to see the world and be seen by other prominent guys. The platinum blonde that I was had indeed caught people's eyes. Although, I agree, I found some of those men very appealing; to me, it was only business. Business, that's it that's all.

I was well aware that I was not the only girl involved in such extra activities. Many other dancers were taking advantage of the wealthy presence around. So, they were kneeling, bending and lying down, as I did. Well, I am not trying to get the public forgiveness here. Not at all. I take full responsibility for me being what I was. Anyhow, that's what we did in those days. The thing is: we were good-looking, we were young, we were body smart and we had the stuff. A moneymaker, that is!

It never occurred to me that it was some sort of prostitution. We were not hookers, we were not escorts. The way I saw it then: we were females enjoying good sex and sharing those pleasures with men who were eager to share something with us. Something called cash. We were girls having fun and making money at the same time, that's it and that's all.

Nonetheless, along with those pleasures, there was a big problem: the chemical. We were put in front of abundance in every way. All kind of substances were at our disposition all the time. We often went to wealthy folks' parties. Pots and snow were offered freely and profusely. That was temptation, as strong as it could be. People on drugs sometimes seemed to blaze up, and that was rather enticing. But I'd remembered my parents' advices against narcotics and I'd never failed. My principle: « Jenny, you will touch none of that! ». Unfortunately, many of us couldn't resist trying, and they got trapped. Courtney, my long time friend, was one of them. She had started and could not quit. So I once told her:

— Courtney, you should stop, you know.

— Stop what?

— Doing drugs.

— Come on, Jen, you've got to know me better than that!

— Seriously Courtney, you've got to stop!

— Come on, girl, don't you worry!

— Of course, I am worried.

— Listen, I'm not a child; I know what I'm doing.

— Still, I think you should stop now.

— Girl, I told you: don't worry! Believe me, I'll stop when I choose to.

Yet it seemed to me that she was hooked and that she was kidding herself. Anyway, I'd said what I had to say. I could do nothing more.

Takisha and her baseball player were still in love. The relationship was going strong; it was getting serious. They were even talking about marriage.

— But, what about your career? Courtney had asked.

— What career?

— As a dancer.

— You know, Court, in a few years, we will be 30 years old! There isn't much place for a 30 years old dancer.

— What are you talking about?

— I'm saying that we have to plan our after-career right now.

— Is it why you are planning to marry Jack?

— Listen to me, Courtney. I am marrying Jack because I love him.

— And because he's wealthy.

— Wealth is not a disease, girls.

— Oh my God, don't we know that!

One month later, Courtney came and announced us she was leaving New Jersey. She was going to live in California. Someone was offering her a part in a movie and she wanted to take that chance. I guess she had probably thought about that after-career plan Takisha talked about. I was happy for her but, at the same time, I felt so miserable. I felt I was losing my closest friends and I was really sad.

But life went on, as usual. I continued dancing and taking care of my business. Though among all the men I encountered, there were some rowdy characters too. One of them would take me to expensive restaurants and would start toying with my body under the table, while we were eating. Another one often asked me to unzip and stroke his privates as he was driving his car. I also met one guy who was so obsessed by the thought of diseases that he'd only wanted me to expose myself in dirty poses and to watch him managing his own pleasure.

Somehow I had found these odd adventures very exciting and, as I said, I was at the same time taking care of business. The gold digging business, that is. Many girls were doing the same. I once had the freakish idea to let my fellow dancers know about my state of mind: « Quench my body and fill up my pocket! », I had said. That had made them laugh out loud. Thus, I had felt confident to persist in speaking openly about it. I told them some of those stories about the weirdos I had met, and after that I added:

— Well, ladies, all a man has to do: show me the money and then throw me the bone. I'll handle everything.

It was obviously a horrible thing to say, I know. Such vulgarity from a woman's mouth! But we were just a bunch of girls having fun at a party. There had been a lot of drinking going on, and many concupiscent males had come after us. So, we were cracking jokes about those men when I let out that "throwing bone" obscenity. I had expected it to be my contribution to the gags. Except that nobody laughed. They all stood in silence, as if they were some offended virgins. Oh, damned hypocrites! Thinking about that night, I realize I was in fact telling my truth; but also I was unveiling theirs, which was: you could be black, you could be white, or any color in between, as long as you were able to spend big, we'd be all around you. My truth: I was a bitch and had only money on my mind. Their truth: they were exactly like I was.

You perhaps remember the time when people of different races didn't mingle. It wasn't long ago. In fact, still in certain circles, that kind of intolerance remains blatant. But then, from where I stood, it seemed to me there was no black or no white anymore. There was only one rule: Money. There were those who had it and those who didn't; that's it that's all.

Thus, my fellow dancers stood in silence. It was an awkward moment. Then one of the girls said to the other girls without smiling, without looking at me:
— Jenny is something else!
Even with a few drinks in my head, I knew right away there would be consequences. Those girls were about to rumor and influence the public opinion against me. Public opinion is the way people who know you think of you, the way they

feel you; which could result in great esteem or total rejection. Public opinion can be manipulated very easily; it doesn't even take a great intelligence to do so. It's all about spreading rumors. It's like a marketing campaign pro or cons a celebrity, a politician, a government, a group of people, a race, a country, a social class, or even simple individuals like you and me. And, that night, I was certain a small scale public opinion manipulating machine was launched.

After three years in that business, I had seen a lot and I had understood a lot. Whatever I had thought about us feeling rich in our New Jersey house was now contradicted. I had realized that we were just very poor people, insignificant people with a too big idea of themselves. I guess that's what the relativity principle is all about: you will define or assess a situation differently, depending on which angle you are beholding it. Thus, I was feeling low and small; so I kept working at having more and much more money. As long as I was beautiful, I knew that I could get going. I just had to be aware of the many threats around and be very cautious. There were too many perverts and there were also diseases. So I was extremely careful.

I must have been good in what I was doing because I'd accumulated lots of cash. I had stopped counting altogether. When you earn much more than you need, there is no urge to count. In spite of my generous contributions at home and my extravagant expenses, my bank account was in the six figures. Even my father, after a life of hard labor, didn't have the tenth of what I had. Let's say, I was kind of proud. But, at the same time, there was something sad: father had been so decent, honest, conscientious and loyal; he had worked to his death. What kind of world was that? Was there some sort of lesson to be learned?

Perhaps, that reflection had prompted me to keep on doing what I was doing. There was no way I would accept to kill myself, working for peanuts. Sometimes, recalling what Takisha had said about a dance career, I had tried to envision what I would become after getting out of the dance field. I must admit I was a little bit nervous.

One Sunday, we all went to church, Arlene, mother and me. Well, I had missed a few Sundays; I was no more part of the steady flock. But I enjoyed very much the sacred moment spent in God presence. I've always been a firm believer in the Scriptures and in prayers, although I was kind of losing faith in some Christians' integrity.

We were about to leave, following the service, when the pastor's wife obviously rushed to us.

— How are you, Barbara? She asked.

— Good, thank you Judy, and you?

— Good, good. How did you find the service today?

— It was great, as usual; don't you agree?

— I don't know; I sensed a lack of energy in the attendance. But maybe I worry too much. You know, my husband and I are not getting any younger.

— This is not true, Judy…

— Well, well. But, enough of me! Look at your beautiful daughters; they are all grown up now.

— Yes. And they've grown so fast too! It seems like yesterday, they were little children…

— Like yesterday, really. Now Arlene has become a very attractive and dependable young woman and Jenny is… Well, Jenny is something else, isn't she?

Mom did not answer. She remained all silent while Judy kept pointing issues about the church. She kept nodding and smiling, as if the pastor's wife words were the only absolute truth. To me, Judy was just a human being, as anybody else. So, I was just eager to get back home and take care of my own business. My mother finally decided to cut off the compulsive blah blah. Still smiling, she said goodbye and quietly left.

But when we got home, my mom lashed out.

— What on earth is wrong with you, Jenny?

— What's wrong with me, mam?

— Don't you see how you dress?

— What is it, with the way I dress?

— What is it? What is it? Don't you have a mirror? You look trashy, that's what it is!

From that moment, I knew that my mother had fully recovered. But I also knew it was about time for me to go away and start living on my own terms. I wasn't a kid anymore and I would definitely not stand to be treated like one.

Something else had impelled me to flee the New Jersey area, as soon as possible. It came to my knowledge that some of the dancers were labeling me with nasty names behind my back. They had decided to call me Jennytals! And it was a laughing matter to everyone. But then, to me, that was pretty hurtful.

Therefore I was more and more determined to leave. It was clear that I was not appropriate for New Jersey anymore. The people there were seeing me in a whole different light; they did not understand at all what I had turned out to be. To them, I had become something else, something strange, something they would not even dare use words to qualify.

6

Courtney had e-mailed us from California. She was in Los Angeles and everything was great. According to her, life was fine over there if you were good enough as an artist and if you had the right contacts. Courtney had indeed fulfilled those two requirements. So she had been regularly working as a dancer. She had let us know that the money was quite interesting. That money factor certainly got my attention. What was remarkable: she got a little part in a movie, and she was even anticipating she'd be called for a more significant role one of these days. She also found herself a new boyfriend who had promised to open for her all the doors to success.

I told mom I was offered an opportunity in California, that sort of opportunity someone could not refuse. I felt guilty lying to my mother,

61

but in fact it was half a lie since I truly believed in the great possibilities ahead.

So I finally left. Mom was very sad, of course. But I suspected she had somehow felt relieved since I'd be carrying away my shameful self out of the neighborhood. It had been hard for her to see me changing in a way which displeased everyone in the vicinity. At least, she had Arlene, the perfect daughter.

I joined Courtney in the middle of January, leaving behind a cold nasty weather. I had wanted to spend Christmas with my mom and Arlene; I thought that might have been our last Holidays together. I arrived in Los Angeles; it was warm and sunny. All was exactly how Courtney had described: cheerful, dynamic and cultural. On my way to her apartment, I was particularly ecstatic when she showed me the Walt Disney Concert Hall, a symbol of the Renaissance that had taken place in the center of Los Angeles. It was an invigorating moment. I felt as if I was on another planet, another world where everything was possible, good or bad. And

I was confirmed instantly that I would never ever go back to live in New Jersey.

Thus I was in California, the State from which came so many outstanding performers. I could not help myself remembering the 2Pac featuring Dr Dre's video for "California Love". I was a teenager when it was released. I recalled watching Dr Dre shaking it then; he was so wildly sexy that I was trembling inside out. In those days, perhaps there was no need for nudity as now; yet the sex-appeal in hip-hop was rising all bystanders' temperatures.

Courtney had a one bedroom apartment. It was small but very beautiful. I had figured out right away that this place was very expensive. I had learned afterward that the price to live there was far beyond whatever I could have presupposed.

Courtney invited me to stay with her freely, the time I would find my own place. But I insisted to contribute to the monthly payments for the rent and all the other expenses which would come up.

Later on, I met Fern, Courtney's boyfriend. He'd taken us to some lavish restaurant, in downtown Los Angeles. It was really cool: the food was excellent and Fern had a way to put everybody at ease. Nevertheless, I was rather astounded. The guy was in his late fifties and wasn't in the least handsome. However, I soon enough understood how important the man would be in Courtney's life: he was rich, he was generous and he knew all the right people, those who'd be willing to make a bright future for her. It takes someone like that sometimes to help soaring oneself up to the stars.

At the beginning, I was all excited and full of hope. I took a few weeks' vacation, just to get acquainted to the new environment and culture. It seemed to me that the Angelenos had a different approach of living. The people appeared sexier there than in the Teaneck area; more beautiful but in a natural way. They obviously were overly conscious about their health and shape. Their preoccupations seemed to tend toward body perfection, skin or hair faultlessness rather than makeup and jewelry. They had that kind of elegance veiled with a touch of nonchalance. It was clear everybody wanted to look fresh and sexy without giving the impression they'd worked too hard at it. Obviously the proximity with Hollywood has a great influence on the customs and the people there.

So I spent part of that vacation touring the LA area. Of course, there was no way I could miss visiting some popular attractions like the Walk of Fame on Hollywood Boulevard, the Universal Studios, the Venice beach and skaters, the palm trees garden and other outdoor sculptures next to the Los Angeles County Museum of Art. There was so much to see; however I had to start thinking of finding work.

I then started to look for a dance assignment. And that's when I realized that all wasn't going to be cool. I was searching intensively, yet there was no result, not even a possibility. After a month, it was clear to me that finding any job here was going to be really difficult. I thought it'd be a good thing to explain the situation to Fern. As I told him about my worries, he assured me he was ready to help me. But, while he was talking, he was kind of stroking my thigh, which I am sure Courtney had noticed. And from that day, I could sense it, she was on her guard. Hence I decided it was time for me to move away.

I had spent a lot of time and energy hunting for a dwelling. The necessary procedures had been tough. In the end, my efforts had paid off; I had found a place. It was a small, ugly and expensive apartment, but at least it was mine. Now it was urgent for me to find a job; I would have to keep taking care of my expenses: the rent, the food and the monthly installments on the car I had bought. I went out a few times with Courtney, running from club to club, hoping I would myself dig up a man to help me launch my career in LA. Well, believe it or not, there was no one for me.

Six months later, I was still looking and couldn't find anything. My savings were thinning rapidly; as things were going now, I would soon be at the end of my rope.

I'd never tried to compare Courtney's easy start with my difficult debut. Obviously, she was having it good, but I didn't have to question whether Courtney had the means to live the way she was. The caliber of her boyfriend explained it all. He was providing for her, big time. That made all the difference. Nonetheless, she had been willing to help me without reservation, and I'd be forever grateful.

So I was now busy running the agencies and auditioning. But the response was always the same: « no »; sometimes politely justified, but sometimes surprisingly brutal. I started to believe I was inadequate. Or that perhaps someone like me, coming from the East Coast, was not welcome in the West Coast. Except that LA was one great metropolis after New York City. There were people from a large variety of countries. Why on earth should I feel so rejected? I guess I didn't know what to think anymore. I was desperate.

Thus I was questioning myself. All kind of stupid ideas came to my mind. However, I remained disciplined: I exercised every day and I practiced all the new moves I'd seen on television. I was practicing all the time lest I should lose my skills as a dancer. And then, as none of the steps I took proved to be effective, I started to pray. I was beginning to believe that God had abandoned me, but I continued to pray anyway; that was the only thing that would keep me going, the only thing that was in my power to do. Since I didn't have a network in LA, I had no hope of meeting wealthy men who could've helped. Well, of course, I had seen lots of beautiful girls standing along Sunset Boulevard, regularly waiting for clients. But I surely didn't wanna become a prostitute.

Meanwhile, the sun was endlessly shining; the flow of joyful tourists was as usual pouring in LA; the spectacular cars with dazzling rims and blasting beats speakers were proudly wandering the streets. But none of those things could have cheered me up, at this point in my life.

By September, I was pretty miserable. There was a heat wave that didn't seem to wanna stop. A blazing fire was consuming the California woods for many days now. The smog was affecting my respiratory capacity; it was difficult for me to practice dancing as I wanted. I was almost certain I was losing my skills and that I would never perform again. The possibility of going back to

New Jersey then crossed my mind. Yeah, I really was in a dire situation.

One afternoon, I was analyzing myself in the mirror, wondering if I was still an attractive woman, when it occurred to me that I could push my style a little bit further. It was probably all about the hair. « Everything's in the hair »; that's what Juanita used to say. And suddenly, I knew exactly what I was going to do.

I took an appointment with one of the best hairdressers I could afford, and I called a style counselor. I was sure those proceedings would be very costly. But I was also sure it would be a great investment.

The price I had to pay for those experts had dramatically surpassed my expectation. I was about to spend the rest of my money on this; it was outrageous! But I was determined to go on anyway; and I did not back out.

There I was on my way to audition again. I felt totally confident. I had taken a good look at myself before leaving my apartment. What I saw in the mirror was a very glamorous and sexy young lady, with the right touch of nonchalance. No one could ever imagine that I had worked too hard at my appearance. I looked just naturally beautiful. I was in full conformity with LA's taste and I was just gorgeous, for real.

My investment had indeed been profitable. I had obtained that first job in LA. And, for whatever reason, I was sure it wouldn't be the last.

That first job! Oh well, it was with a female young singer. I had thought it would be a soft and agreeable way to begin my career in LA, but believe it or not, that girl was so aggressive and disrespectful that I truly felt I should quit the job right in the middle of it. That girl would scream insanities and throw tantrum after tantrum. No one on earth should be working in conditions like that. However, I really needed the money and, above all, I needed to prove I was reliable; so I had to endure her wicked way. In fact, the whole crew had to endure as well. Our only consolation was that we were all aware that every one of us hated her. Just knowing that fact actually helped us.

To my dismay, when the video came out later on the screens, that awful brat appeared so beautiful and sexy and likable! I guess I was taught another life lesson: the devil bears occasionally the adorable face of an angel!

7

It sometimes takes a great haircut to alter the course of a life. My new hairdo was very short and extremely sexy. It was one of those asymmetrical Pixie cuts, with silky side bangs. I was still a platinum blonde, but with beautifully forged darker roots. That hairdresser was an expert; I already said that, I know. As a result, I had found myself a good agent and I was offered dance contracts steadily. So, my intention was to keep that fantastic new look for a very long time.

More than one year had passed since I was in LA and all was going well. I was earning enough money to live, to have fun and to save. My life was quite satisfying. I had resumed dating, but only every now and then; I didn't want to be called Jennytals ever again.

During that period, I had encountered many girls. Most of them seemed pretty amiable and cool. But I'd been burned before; so I showed to everyone my most affable face but kept my distance at all times. I was in no hurry to make new friends. However, I did keep in touch with enough acquaintances for Saturday night's parties and other exciting events purposes.

Courtney was on her way to success. She was part actor part dancer, and she was making a lot of money. Her boyfriend was opening doors, for sure. So she was very busy and was always running to something new. It was difficult to even talk to her on the phone. One of these days Courtney was gonna be a star; I had no doubt about that.

Takisha was to be married in two months. Jack was pretty much in love. The wedding would take place in New York and I was determined to attend, unless, of course, a very important obligation would have occurred.

My recent assignments were mostly with female artists. That was to me a very different dynamic.

73

I probably had preferred working with the masculine energy, although we'd been paid well in either scenario. Still, I was hoping that I'd be backing-up some famous hip-hop male artist in the near future. My wish was granted a few months later, just after I had returned from New York.

I had promised that I would attend Takisha's wedding and I did. It was a magnificent ceremony with loads of beautiful flowers and a sumptuous reception. Takisha looked as a true princess in her majestic white gown. Jack and Takisha formed a striking couple. And you could feel the joy all around them and in them. Yes, their happiness was utterly genuine that day.

I went to New Jersey to visit my mom and my sister. Both of them were in good shape. Mother was happy to see me, but could not understand why I had cut my hair. Arlene, on the contrary, said I was stunning. She was dating a sales director in a very good company. Henry, my sister's boyfriend seemed a very nice person and he was handsome too. He had just completed a Master degree in Business. Curiously, those few hours with my family will remain in my memory as a very special moment. I found myself regretting to leave them so fast. I guess I was renewing with a comforting feeling of security that I wouldn't find anywhere else, knowing that my mom and my sister Arlene were the only persons I could completely trust.

So I was kind of nostalgic when I returned to LA. I kept on thinking of that time when things were simple and satisfying. And now that I've learned another way of life, there would certainly be no turning back.

I was in a somber mood when my agent called me that afternoon. There was a video shooting starting next week, and the artist was no one but the prominent rapper called Da-Steel. I should probably be ashamed to say that all the sad thoughts about my past had vanished when I heard the name Da-Steel. It was that kind of opportunity I would not even dare anticipate. That was, to me, as a great miracle and I was soon jumping up and down with joy.

I then felt so great I decided I would go shopping on Robertson Boulevard. I'd probably buy some clothes or whatever fantastic stuff I would find on my way. As I do often, when I go shopping I like to wear very nice and sexy outfits. So I was not intimidated when I entered the Chanel boutique. I was there for about five minutes, looking at one very pricey purse when a sophisticated black lady with a strong British accent approached me.

— Ravishing, is it not?

— Definitely ravishing.

I had answered with my coolest voice tone, as if Chanel bags were something I purchased every day. In reality, I'd never owned a single one. Of course, like all the other girls, I was dreaming of having a great collection of them. But I had always thought such articles were the kind of things only wealthy men would offer as gifts to a girlfriend or a mistress. So I was amazed when she asked the salesman for two different colors of that same excruciatingly costly bag.

I was about to leave the boutique when that young woman came to me again.

— I am Mariam, she said.

— I'm Jennifer.

— Do you live in Los Angeles, Jennifer?

— Yes, I do. And you?

— I would really like to live here, I think. But, no, I live in London.

— So you're here in vacation?

— I believe you could say so. A very short vacation, though. One of my friends is having a birthday party, and here I am.

— You mean you came just for a birthday party?

— But of course. Don't you approve?

— I don't know. It seems a long way to travel just for a party.

— Of course not! We do that all the time.

— But how do you manage with your work?

— Work!? Did you say "work"?

— Yes: W O R K, I spelled.

— Oh really?

— Yeah.

— But I do not work; do you?

At this moment, it hit me that I might've been talking to one of those rich African girls, the kind who have a multimillion dollars dad. I quickly told myself that I was on the wrong path with that conversation. I remembered once hearing that, for some wealthy folks, to work was like something dirty, something too low, totally unconceivable for their class. So what was I going to respond to her «Do you?»?

— It happens sometimes.

That was my answer. But I managed to sound nonchalant enough. I looked at her without blinking. I concocted on my face some sort of candid smile which, in fact, wasn't candid at all.

— Oh God! And what do you do?

— I am a dancer.

And, to my surprise, Mariam suddenly became really enthusiastic. Often rich people are proved to be very fond of artists; it's a fact. I guess I somehow knew I would earn her admiration when I said I was a dancer. At this stage, she was so thrilled she turned to me and said.

— Then, you've got to come to the party with me tomorrow night.

— To the party with you? But I don't even know these people.

— "These people", as you call them, are my friends.

— So?

—So my friends are their friends too.

— I don't usually crash people party.

— Would you mind if we discussed this over a coffee!

It turned out Mariam was not the kind of girl who would take "no" as an answer. And there I was, the day after, entering one of those fabulous whereabouts. It was that sort of mansion usually hidden from public eyes by tall trees and a five minutes drive after one was granted access at a solid wrought iron gate.

We had agreed that her chauffeur would pick me up in the evening. Luckily, a few months before, I had bought a very sexy dress that had cost me half an arm. It had been hanging in the closet since, and I had been wondering if I'd ever have an occasion to wear it. That dress looked quite sober in the front, but was cut very low in the back. Being a classical dancer in my younger age had given me a queenly bearing that everyone admired. So I was aware that my new dress along with my short hairdo would beautifully uncover my nape and back.

By nine o'clock, a Rolls Royce was waiting for me right in front of my home. I was very intimidated. Mariam was sitting in the back when I got in the car. She was rather casual, but magnificent at the same time. Just one look at her had confirmed that she was indeed a multimillion dad's daughter. Only a very wealthy girl could wear tenth of thousands of dollars outfits so nonchalantly.

I must admit I was a little bit shaky inside, though I tried to appear relaxed. And then Mariam smiled at me, as if I was a long time friend; that made me feel comfortable. However, I got anxious again when we passed the large gate and drove through the dense wood. I started to think that I could as well disappear for good, as I was a girl living alone in LA. You know, this world can be a dreadful place sometimes. So all kind of « What if…? » came to my mind.

We finally found ourselves in a hall decorated with flowers, statuettes, large paintings and luxurious hangings. I had never seen such a high ceiling! That was incredible. To me, it was like suddenly leaving the world I knew for some phantasmagorical site. I just could not believe that kind of opulence existed. To me, entering that mansion was a crucial moment, the moment

I realized I was simply a nobody, and that all the stuff I used to believe expensive or dazzling were nothing else but junk.

We crossed an interior yard and fell right into the party. We were now in an immense room flanked by two mezzanines full of animated people. It was a young horde as any young horde anywhere; except most of them were very rich. Everybody was dancing, drinking or doing something fun.

Mariam went to her friend, a reddish hair blue eyes good-looking guy in a gray T-shirt and worn-out blue-jeans. Steven was his name. « Happy birthday, Stevie! » she shouted. There were kisses and laughs and kisses again.
— Steven, here's my friend Jennifer!
— Happy birthday, I told him.
— Thanks. Welcome to my party! Mariam's friends are my friends.

I just smiled. There was nothing else to say. From that moment on, I felt at home. We went to the bar and got ourselves a few drinks. Many maids dressed in sexy black outfits with delicate white aprons were carrying trays of goodies. We were

81

offered caviar and fancy cocktail-snacks. The Champagne was flowing along the other spirituous liquors. We ate a little but we drank a lot. Then we mingled in the crowd, on what was supposed to be the dance floor. Some African music was now playing, a strange and loud music with beats and rhythms to conquer your spirit and drive you wild. No possible way for anybody to resist. I did not even try. I let myself get high on the music and danced as if there was no tomorrow. Yeah, that's what I did. That's what everyone did. That's what this great birthday party was all about.

I got home at dawn. I was exhausted, but yet I was still feeling high. My mind was wandering around, revisiting all the details of that night at Steven's. I just understood that another kind of life existed and that I wasn't in it.

Two days later, Mariam and I met for coffee on Robertson Boulevard. She was leaving in less than 24 hours and we promised that we would keep contact. We were sitting on a flowery terrace contiguous with an elegant restaurant. And, of course, Mariam fitted well with the place. I could not help noticing her Hermes bag which I knew for a fact might have cost her not far from 100 000$! Yeah, Mariam was indeed a very wealthy girl.

8

The shooting was going well. We had practiced enough, the previous days. We were a bunch of experienced female dancers and remarkable male breakers. The music was tremendous and Da-Steel was a terrific performer. There was no doubt in my mind: that video was gonna be awesome.

As usual, all the girls were playing their little game, trying to catch the artist attention. Every one of them was convinced to be the chosen, the future Da-Steel's official girl; so they were keeping an eye on each other, ready to defend a territory they were not about to own. Nora, a French girl who grew up in LA told us she had worked with Da-Steel before, and that they had a little something going on. I guess it was her way

trying to shut the door on any aspirants' expectation. But anyway, none of us believed her.
— I'm so damn tired of those BMW! muttered Joanna, a gorgeous black girl and a great dancer.

I knew exactly what she meant. I was well aware that BMW stood for Black Male Female, in reference to white women dating mostly black men. And Nora was indeed one of these.

Da-Steel was a dark-skinned, easy on the eye man; the kind of man any woman would find attractive, even if he had been an ordinary guy. But, on top of being good-looking, he was a famous hip-hop artist and he was very rich, making him a perfect target for gold diggers around the globe. Da-Steel would only have to snap his fingers for any girl anywhere to rush in an attempt to please him. So I was in a state of shock when, the first afternoon, I saw Da-Steel walking toward me and heard him ask:
— Hey yo, weren't you at Steven's party?
— Oh, yes I was. Were you there?
— How do you think I know you were there?
— Yeah, obviously, you were there.
— It was a great party, wasn't it?

— Absolutely.

— Well then, see you.

— OK.

That was all we said that day. But from that instant, I was walking on air. I kind of detected Nora standing not too far, looking askance at me. However I could not process any negative thought at that moment. I was going into raptures over the fact that Da-Steel and I were at the same party and that he'd noticed me!

The next day we didn't talk at all. He seemed barely aware of my presence. I was hoping he'd at least say hello; but he didn't. You see, I was anticipating nothing more. From that episode with JupitA, I knew exactly what I represented for those guys. And I had learned my lesson well. What was I to expect from a young man who had the most beautiful women at his feet?

Yet, the third day, Da-Steel came to me again.

— How are you doing? he asked.

— Good, I whispered.

Let's say I could barely talk; I was hypnotized. Da-Steel was extremely polite, but that didn't help at all. I was agitated inside, scatterbrained. And though I was trying to appear collected, it was certain he felt my nervousness.

— What are you doing later on?

— Don't know yet.

— Could I invite you to the restaurant, if you're available?

— Yes, of course, I'd like that.

Not one second, it had occurred to me to say no. Juanita had once explained: « strategically, the right dose of caprice, a touch of coquetry, a feigned indifference; these are attitudes which could add a lot to a girl's worth ». But I've never been a playing hard to get type of girl. Instead, I capitulated right away.

Thus, we went out that evening. Steel was the perfect gentleman. I just could not believe that such a prominent artist appeared so simple and graceful; I was used to those arrogant and overconfident ones. That night was definitely the best moment in my life. I really thought I was dreaming: Da-Steel was such a fine man and he was truly kind with me. Yes, for sure, Da-Steel was THE man. And I was in Heaven.

Then, on the fourth day, the accident happened. The filming was almost over and all was going well. I was practicing one of those risky moves where I had to jump and flip at the same time. I probably wasn't in my best shape: eventually, I did not sleep the night before; I had been thinking of Da-Steel. In fact, I was again and again recollecting our conversation in the restaurant while I was performing, until I fell and hit the ground.

All happened too quickly. The b-boys had just completed some acrobatic steps; the girls were starting their dance part. So I was about to flip when I realized that Nora was coming a little too close to me. To tell the truth, that's all I remember. As soon as I hit the floor, I knew I was in big trouble. There are no words to describe the kind of pain you undergo when a bone is broken. I was roaring; there was no way I could restrain my screams. That was a horrible moment. The ambulance arrived and took me to the hospital where I was confirmed that my arm would be out of order for many weeks. That was really awful: my body was my tool, my moneymaker; so I was very concerned. I was afraid my dance career would never be the same, following that ordeal. I'd be out of practice for a long time; there was no guarantee I could ever catch up after that. My life was taking a bad turn.

But all my worries vanished like a snow flake in the sun when Da-Steel entered my room carrying a large bouquet. He came at the hospital to visit me, the day after I fell. He came again the day after, and every other day that I spent there, bringing flowers each time. That man was definitely a class act.

During those visits, we had talked a lot. It was so easy to be with him. It was as if we had known each other since childhood. Believe it or not, in spite of my broken arm, those were the sweetest days of my entire life. I never thought I could open my heart to a man as I did with Da-Steel while I was an in-patient. He might have felt he was experiencing something special also, because he had revealed so much about himself to me. Hence I learned that his first name was in fact Amadeus, as in Wolfgang Amadeus Mozart. His parents might've had a presentiment that he was destined to become a star in the music industry.

Some people would have found that laughable; to me, it was rather a very touching story, even though I had decided to call him just Steel.

I spent four days in all, at the hospital. When it was the moment to leave, Steel was right there for me; he had proposed to pick me up and take me to my home. So, our relationship had started for good. There was no doubt in my mind: we were definitely on solid ground.

Courtney had visited me twice at the hospital. I was very happy to see her, and also very surprised because of her busy schedule. But, imagine my amazement to see her after that, coming to my apartment on a daily basis, just to help in whatever I was doing. And I had to thank the Lord for giving me such a loyal friend and for allowing her to accompany me through difficult periods. However, I started to feel guilty for being the cause of any potential delay in her many projects.

— Courtney I am so grateful for all you've done for me. But, you know, your career is the most important thing right now; you should really take care of your business.

— You're my best friend, Jenny. I won't leave you all alone in that mess.

— I am not that alone, you know. Don't worry, I'll manage!

— Come on, you'd do the same for me.

— But what about your work?

— Oh everything is fine, actually! I took a little vacation; I needed that, really.

Of course, by coming to see me, she had to meet Steel many times. Let's say I was rather proud to show her that such a celebrity was a friend of mine. Da-Steel was working at other videos for his newest album but would visit me between whiles. Courtney would stay as long as he was there and she would be joking around with him, which seemed pretty normal to me.

Meanwhile I had received a few calls and several emails from Mariam. She was always travelling somewhere. I could not understand that one person had so many acquaintances. From my point of view, managing all those relationships seemed a heavy burden. But, I suppose, to Mariam, it was simple routine.

More than two weeks had passed. Courtney was still visiting regularly. She would usually spend the whole afternoon with me. And then, one day, she came to me with an unexpected request.

— Gilrfriend, would you agree if I stayed with you for a while?

— You mean: stay, as to move in here with me?

— Yeah. But it'd be for a few days.

— Well, of course, Courtney… But, you realize it's very small here?

— Thank you, Jenny! Thank you so much.

How could I possibly say no to the girl who had sheltered me during my first weeks in LA? Again I felt I was ungrateful, because I was not too eager at the idea. And I felt even worst when I forced myself to smile broadly, in order to show some enthusiasm while concluding:

— It's gonna be a lot of fun.

Later, Courtney explained that she had had an argument with Fern and that she was pretty upset. She needed to take a few days away from him, in order to reflect on her future. She was certain however that they would soon resolve their differences, like all lovers usually do.

So Courtney moved in. And, from that moment, I regretted having said yes. The nice empathetic girl who had showed so much concern for me was no more. It was a quick and surprising transformation. One minute, she was all sweet and playful; the next minute, she was barking insults to everybody, me included. A new Courtney was rising, filled with arrogance, anger and hostility.

And then, she started to go out at night. She would dress exaggeratedly sexy and put on her high heels; she would curtly say «Bye» and she would be out there until morning. Obviously, something strange was going on. Courtney would spend the day sleeping. She would wake up late in the afternoon, she would openly indulge herself in all kind of narcotics consumption and she would resume acting recklessly until she'd be out again. There was no remaining trace of our friendship. Courtney would talk on a harsh tone through her clenched teeth. On her face, there was always an awkward disdaining look which was dedicated to me. I could not understand why she suddenly seemed to hate me, and I was wondering if I had inadvertently hurt her feelings.

I was analyzing all my previous behaviors and the conversations we had, trying to spot anything bad I would have said or done. But I couldn't find anything. Nevertheless, she was overtly hostile toward me and I really began to dislike her.

Curiously, in the presence of Steel, there was the very pleasant Courtney again. She'd welcome him with laughter, touching him in an overly friendly way, taking suggestive postures and trying to be the focus of his attention. I was looking at her and just could not believe my eyes. I told myself she surely didn't know she was acting phony. So it seemed normal to me to ask her about her feelings.

— You really like Steel, don't you?

— What do you mean?

— I mean: don't you like Steel?

— What is that question all about? Is he your boyfriend?

— No, he's not.

— Well then, keep your freakin' questions to yourself !

— Why do you have to be that rude?

— Excuse-me?

— Why do you have to be so rude?

— So I am the rude one now! Why don't you look at your own self? Don't you find it rude to ask me stupid questions like you just did?

— OK, Courtney, you know what?

— What?

— Who the hell are you? I don't even recognize the friend you said you were!

— Why don't you just shut up, Jennifer?

— Yeah, you're right. Let's not speak to each other until you leave my apartment!

— Fuck you, Jennifer!

I really felt like slapping her in her face. Nevertheless, I did nothing; with my plastered arm, it would be so easy for her to beat the crap out of me. Instead, I turned away from her and went on taking care of my business. From that moment on, we did not talk at all. We did not even look at each other, until the time she left.

Meanwhile Steel was coming every day and Courtney was being friendlier toward him; so much so, I felt I had to take a certain distance. They were becoming so close; it seemed to me that I was the intruder in a relationship that was their own. Believe me, that was quite painful; I had really thought Steel was a special friend to me, but Courtney appeared to have now a privileged access to him. It was clear that I had to back off. Yeah, that was very hard: we were sharing such a small space, I couldn't help myself seeing them kidding around all the time. Definitely, Courtney's presence was a huge and constant source of stress for me.

And then, the Da-Steel videos were completed. Now the promoting activities were on. I knew they would consume all his time and effort. He was going to travel a lot and there was no guarantee I would ever see him again. A few weeks before, I was convinced we were friends; well, I admit I wasn't so sure anymore.

After five weeks, the cast was taken off my arm. After I left the hospital, it occurred to me suddenly that I was breathing and biting in a beautiful day. Truly, it was a marvelous moment. I would never know that happiness could result from such simple events, if I hadn't lost the use of my arm for such a long time. And now, being able to sleep freely, to take a bath easily, and suffering no more from those exasperating itches on my skin; that was a pure delight. And I prayed God that day to let me remember that happiness was as simple as that.

So here I was again. I knew I had to take some other steps before I could resume my regular activities, but still, I felt so great. I was ready to do whatever it would take to get better, and to get better fast.

However, as the days went by, I started to feel down again. Courtney's presence didn't help, for sure. I was thinking of Steel who had called us from time to time. I was sure he was forgetting that we once had such a special friendship, and I was trying to teach myself to forget him too.

I had to go through physiotherapy sessions in order to recommence dancing. I was anxiously waiting to be able to perform again. I had not worked for a long time and I had paid huge amounts of money in medical fees. In spite of previous good intentions, my future appeared to me pretty blurred. Really, I was in a dull mood; it seemed that my life was falling apart once again.

Fortunately, a month later, Courtney moved out. It was a big relief. I don't think I could have supported her company much longer. Perhaps we would have ended that relationship with a violent fight. But, believe it or not, she took the time to say goodbye and to thank me; she even gave me a hug and a kiss on each cheek. Courtney was full of surprises.

9

As I had anticipated, the Da-Steel videos went viral. His music was smashing the dance floors all over the world. You would hear it on your radio, on the homeboy's ghettoblaster, or flying in the air spreading out of a passing car. The videos were featuring on TV many times a day and, most of all, people was buying his CD from everywhere. Steel himself gave no sign of life; I supposed he might have been incredibly busy. Or perhaps he had just forgotten me.

My arm was in a better shape, so I went to my agent, looking for some easy job to start over. He was kind enough to receive me but made sure he didn't waste much time talking with me. It was a very short conversation in which he stated he was pleased to see me on my feet again. And I was thinking « Why talk about my feet while you should rather be asking me for my injured arm? ». But I guess he just didn't really care, even though he was trying to show a bit of solicitude. Five minutes after my arrival, he checked his watch and stood up, signifying that our chat was over.

— Well, Jen, I'll contact you as soon as we have something.

Hence, the following days revealed themselves as a constant series of hope and despair. It was a simple pattern: I regularly woke up with big hope but, as no good news rang my bell, that hope was gradually shifting into desperation as the sunlight declined. The good thing was that I would go to bed and sleep tight all night long. Probably because I had spent many hours every day working out and practicing dance moves.

I kept on checking my phone too many times in the course of that period, hoping to hear from my agent and, above all, longing to hear from Steel. Since he had left, I didn't date anybody. It was as if something in me was broken. There wasn't a single pleasant occasion for me; my life was pretty dull.

Mariam and me kept some sort of friendship. That was rather stressing because there was no way I could ever follow her in her grand lifestyle. She had telephoned every now and then, inviting me to an event or another: a party in Italy, a brunch in Paris or a safari in South Africa. And each time I had to find an excuse. Of course, I was not going to mention that I wasn't a rich daddy's girl. And I did not feel guilty at all; I wasn't hurting anybody by not telling her. But then, at one point, she'd stopped inviting me; she would drop an email from time to time to simply say hello.

After a few weeks, I decided to call my agent every other day. He answered my three first calls and each time repeated those exact same words: « If there's anything, I'll contact you ». After that, the secretary completely blocked my access to him. She really didn't want to put me through. She would say « Mr. Lock is in a meeting » or « Mr. Lock is out for the day ». And, later on, I could feel the impatience in her voice when she announced me « Mr. Lock is out of town » and that she had no idea on the time he was going to be back. I finally understood there was no future for me with that agency, so I decided to go out looking elsewhere. I met a few hustlers proposing me to become an exotic dancer. My response was a plain « NO ». There was no way on earth, really no way I would accept such a degradation, in spite of the fragile financial condition I was in. But then, I was imagining the comments from those who had known me since childhood, my few good friends' disappointment, the hateful sense of victory my enemies would gladly share and, ultimately, the shame and pain I would cause to my family.

Meanwhile, Ludacris "Moneymaker" video was playing on TV all day long. And there I was, considering those big money incentives, the promises coming from an enticing song, and wondering when I would resume shaking mine. At that time of my life, once again, there was no income, only expenses. Big expenses! And the savings I had rebuilt were about to fall flat.

The news arrived, as if I didn't have enough problems: my grandmother was sick. She was diagnosed with breast cancer. She would have to undergo a double mastectomy, and then all the chemotherapy tribulations. That was going to be a very tough period in a 75 years old woman. I wept myself exhausted that day; I loved my grandmother dearly and I was wondering why a woman who had taken such good care of her children and grandchildren had to suffer that much. All the great moment I had spent with her came hunting me. A stream of memories was passing through my mind and also the sound of that Nina Simone's song: "*Black is the color of my true love's hair*" she used to sing while gazing at my grandfather, the man who had been the love of her life and who had died in her arms.

The news about my grandmother had been another blow. For a while, the other problems that I was experiencing seemed small; it was now all about her. Luckily, mom had announced that she planned to spend most of her free time with her. But still, I felt I should return to New Jersey in order to be close to the ones I could totally trust, those who had always given me their love and their undivided affection. Nevertheless, I remained in LA.

Those days in my life had been bad days. I guess I had no inner strength to be able to face those challenges. There was no maxim, not a verse, not a prayer which could bring me a little hope. I was prostrated; I'd only go out for the bare necessities. I had no appetite for enjoyment whatsoever. I could not even stand the Hip-hop music anymore. I guess I was also trying to avoid anything that would make me think of Da-Steel. Thus, I stayed in for many days, contemplating my own defeat while listening to David Bowie, Queen, Guns N'Roses or Aerosmith.

It was now eight months since I had not worked. My situation was critical. I just could not believe the days had gone so fast and that I had done nothing with my life for such a long time. I was panicking; it was a matter of weeks now before I completely ran out of money —16 weeks exactly, if I was cautious. Funny how the thoughts of Steel were fading away, leaving my whole mind to my financial worries!

Thus, I had searched in vain any assignment as a dancer. I had knocked at many doors which remained closed. My acquaintances had deserted me; no more invitations to Saturday nights' parties or other events. At that point, I started to remember the other Nina Simone song my grandmother used to listen to: « *Nobody knows you when you're down and out* ». Hence, I could find no job and I could find no help, no moral support. That meant I had to count on myself and on myself only to get out from that mess. But how?

That was it then: no more assignment for me as a dancer! I knew that sooner or later, I had to look for another option. Rather sooner than later. But what? I had no other work experience; I had quit school with no particular skills. It occurred to me that a store or a boutique would probably hire me, although the salary was going to be insignificant. So I went on offering my services to find myself rejected again and again. So, what now? Was I going to wash the dishes in a restaurant? Was I going to work as a maintenance lady who vacuums carpets and cleans toilet bowls? No, there was no way I was going to go that way. Anything else but that! In desperation, I decided I would revisit those exotic dancers' agencies and finally accepted to work in one of their clubs.

« Only for a little while »; that's what I told myself. « Just to help me gather the money I need, in order to hit upon a more decent occupation ».

So there I was, showing my skin to a throng of male beholders, a pack of horny hounds. Yeah, that was it: the lust business! Beth, one of the girls who had worked in the club for two years explained to me how the financial rewarding would be almost as good as a medical doctor's paycheck, if I was ready to perform extra private dances. But then, it was my first day there; I wasn't in the mood for lust career planning.

There was a very good looking young man who came every evening and stayed at the bar drinking scotch. He was always dressed in expensive businessmen suits; but a heavy gold chain around his neck let me know from the start he was a pimp. That guy was considering me with an obvious interest, probably assessing how much a girl like me would bring to his pocket.

At first, I was ashamed and intimidated by this environment that should not have been mine.

I was a little frightened too, knowing that bad things could occur while I was working there. However, I was mostly humiliated, mortified by my degradation, and afraid that any former acquaintance would one day show up in the club. Such a downfall was undignified enough; I needed no witness on top of that.

But, believe it or not, soon enough I started to get pretty comfortable. Beth's presence had possibly convinced me that I was just fine. She was a gorgeous girl, very modern, wearing pricey designer clothes and carrying herself as a true royalty; the kind of girl —if you had met her on the outside of the club— would give the impression she was a rich heiress. Consequently, it entered my mind that if Beth was so at ease doing that job, it should have been the same for me. That's how the « little while » I had thought I would stay in that job became so easily six months. And I'd probably stay there forever, if something had not abruptly stopped me.

I was dancing and showing myself in sheer nudity for the club's customers, and it appeared to me that their screams and whistles were out of their admiration for my stunning body. It seemed that they were clamoring for me and I was excited that I had such a hold on them. The fear of being recognized rapidly subsided; chances were if an acquaintance of mine had entered the place, that person would be as embarrassed as me and would certainly not like other folks to know they had come there. I was only discreet on my way in or on my way out of the club, as I still didn't wish to disclose that I was part of that type of industry's crew.

As I had once followed Juanita, I was currently following Beth. Everything she said happened to be true; I did all she had suggested and I was making lots of money. After my usual routines, I would go to one of the backstage cubicles and show my stuff to my private clients. In there, I could closely behold the power of a naked girl on any given man. I was new in the place, and they wanted to see as much of me as possible. Beside the regular pay, they would tip my performances by handing to me numerous dollar bills. I could remember Juanita saying « In God and in the dollar bill I trust! » and I was so inclined to agree with her now. In fact, in that exotic dancers' club, money and stuff were the girls' only dreams. It was that same old story over and over: designer clothes, pricey purses, expensive shoes and very wealthy men who could provide those things.

When Beth invited me out for a drink and suggested to introduce me to a few generous men, it didn't occur to me to say no. And I soon resumed dating men for money, in spite of the fact I had previously exhorted myself to stop acting that way. Once again, I was allowing and enjoying weird sexual encounters and, indeed, my bank account was growing fast.

It was one of those nights, the kind of nights when you sense the only fun activity would be to stay at home and watch television. I really didn't feel like going out; but, of course, it was out of question to overlook a very promising date. That rendez-vous —with a man I had seen for the first time the night before— seemed potentially profitable. Thus, I slipped into a very sexy dress, put on my high heels and left home.

Leon was his name. At least, that's how he introduced himself to me. I had met him at a private club Beth used to frequent. It was that king of club you had to pay tenth of thousands of dollars for membership. Beth had made herself friend with the doorman; and that explained how we happened to get in. It goes without saying that the members were very rich gentlemen. And the ladies, well, they were, for the most, women looking for the kind of men who were there.

Leon was a nice man, in his look and his manners. He appeared refined and generous. While he was ordering the drinks, Beth had whispered « Hey, big spender! »; that's how she usually indicated potentially profitable men. I was under the impression she was really interested in him. Nevertheless, Leon had fixed his choice upon me.

As I was heading to meet Leon, once again I felt a strong desire to return home and just relax. But, obviously, there was no way I was going to do that. We had agreed to meet in the same club where we had first seen each other, the previous night. It was a very stylish place and I was rather proud to be part of that elegant crowd.

The night had started well; it was kind of taking a romantic turn and I was glad I came. Leon was a soft-spoken gentleman. He complimented me on my look and ordered a few drinks. He talked about his life, his parents, his past deceptions and his expectations. I must say that his story had genuinely moved me. He asked me many questions on myself; he was so caring and courteous! He listened to my every word, showing his profound interest by nodding from time to time. I felt that he cared; and that was to me a sweet sensation. Leon was so polite and kind that I was ashamed for previously wanting to stay home, what Beth and I used to call « an old lady's attitude ». At one point, I checked out his left hand; there was no wedding ring! So I started to picture a possible future for him and me together.

We left the club around midnight. Leon inquired if I'd like to see where he resides. I was curious, for sure; so I consented to drive there, following his Mercedes-Benz coupé cabriolet. That very expensive car, to me, was another good sign. I knew then I was a lucky girl, and I thought: « Yes, he's the man! ».

It took us at least half an hour to arrive at his dwelling. We entered a private tree-lined road and, two minutes later, there stood a massive house. By then, I was certain the guy was filthy rich.

We went in by a side gate, walked along a corridor and found ourselves in front of a carved wooden door. We got into the room. Surprisingly, three persons were already there: two men and a woman completely naked! It was a startling view and I knew right away I was in deep trouble. « What have I gotten myself into? » I wondered. I quickly turned to Leon and asked:
— What's going on?
I received no answer. I could see in his face that the nice guy I thought he was had changed into something fiendish. His eyes were cold blue, and the stiff smile on his lips was frightful.

The woman was performing oral sex on one of the men, while the other one —who seemed much older— was watching and touching. He stopped fondling her when he saw me; and now he was coming in my direction. I gripped Leon's sleeve; I was in a state of shock. Leon swiftly drew himself away from me, and then he violently pushed me toward the wicked guy. I was in panic and I thought I would not get out alive from that room. The guy grabbed me and I tried to fight him. He easily ripped off my dress. I instinctively started to scream. He then put his filthy hand on my mouth, so I attempted unsuccessfully to bite him. I was fighting like hell and I finally scratched him in his face. That's when he repeatedly hit me with his fist, and I saw flying stars before I fell down on the floor. I understood that it was a matter of life and death; there was nothing I could do to avoid that man to rape me. They all came to me; they forced me to gulp half a bottle of Whisky while they were touching my body in the most intrusive way. I was smashed but I was not unconscious when they carried out many dirty tricks on me. There was no other word to describe that ordeal: torture! Yes, it was torture. Afterward, they all had their turn climbing onto me. And Leon's was the last.

Those bloody assholes were now sleeping like pigs. The other woman was asleep also; she was still naked. I might have dozed off as well. I didn't have any idea what time it could have been. My head felt heavy and there was a buzzing noise in my ears. I could see clearly the place we were in; the daylight was coming from a series of shutters located high on the wall. Everything there indicated money and debauchery. It was pretty obvious the owner was a pervert.

I considered that it was the right moment for me to try to escape. I put back on my ripped dress, got up as silently as I could and walked on the tip of my toes to the door. However, my effort to open it turned out to be ineffective; I was locked in for good. Now I had to hang around until those rascals got up; I was certainly not going to wake them. So I waited, and they finally did.

— I need to go home now. Would you open the door? I said fiercely.

— First you have to sign the contract.

Leon had replied calmly, with an innocent sleepy voice. I just could not believe my ears.

— What contract? I inquired.

— The one offering your services to us.

— But what services? I never offered you anything!

— Come on, now!

— What do you want of me?

— We've already taken whatever we wanted. You just have to sign the contract, as a prostitute having consented to do a certain job for us last night.

— You know damn well this is not true!

— This is the absolute truth.

— Come on, mother fuckers, let me go!

The old guy took a leap toward me and put his face right next to mine. I could smell his morning breath mixed with the alcohol. He placed his fingers all around my neck as an attempt to strangle me. And then he turned, as if he was about to go away. Then he faced me again and slapped me ruthlessly. Once again there were little blue stars flashing before my eyes.

— We fucked no mother; do you hear me? We fucked no mother but YOU bitch, he lashed out.

His face turned all red when he screamed:

— Don't you dare mention mother again!

He then pushed me violently. I collapsed on a couch nearby. I was terrified when I saw him approaching. Was he going to hurt me again? That bastard came close to me. He was flaunting his junk right in front of my mouth and, for a few seconds, I really considered biting in it. But I knew I would end up dead if I did. So, I could not help myself sobbing again:

— Let me go! Please, let me go!

— Not before you sign the contract.

— But I never offered you my services, and I am not a prostitute.

— You mean we have made a mistake?

For a while I thought they were coming to their senses. I kind of felt that I should show some strength, now they were realizing that they had been so wrong. Thus I shouted:

— You have made a big mistake… and you will pay for that!

— Oh yeah? Listen, guys, the whore is threatening us now!

That was the other man who had been watching the scene and hadn't spoken yet.

— Take that slut to the basement! She needs to reflect on the situation, suggested the old man.

— Listen, I just wanna go home!

— Not until you sign.

— Do you mean you're going to keep me here, if I don't?

— You can fucking bet on that, sweetheart!

Now, I was petrified. How many times have you heard about women disappearing? Hence, I was not going to argue anymore; I was ready to give them whatever they were asking for.

As I was about to sign the contract stipulating that I had offered my services as a prostitute for an amount of 5000$, they handed to me personal documents that I usually kept in my car's glove compartment. Leon or some other stooge had previously stolen my papers, which meant they had collected important information about me.

— And don't you even try a fake signature! advised Leon.

10

When I got home that afternoon, I sat down for several hours, trying to appease the storm that was raging in me. I'd looked at myself in the mirror: I was covered in bruises. My skin was sore all over; my body was aching everywhere. Oh My God, I was so damaged! But, what a ridiculous woman I had been! And then I had even considered Leon and myself as a possible match! Lord, what was I thinking?

I did not discard the money. After all, I earned it the hard way. 5000$! That would not buy me enough soap to clean out the dirt lingering on my soul. There was a time when I had received twice as much for enjoying great sex with one attractive man. There was a lesson to be learned, and I had learned it.

Many days had passed before I could function in a regular way. I stayed home, in extreme anxiety. I did not even go out for groceries, did not answer the phone, did not read my emails. It came across my mind to go to the police and press charges. But I rapidly ruled out that idea; attacking those people could be very dangerous. And, besides, I had signed the supposed consent. I had to let it go and allow time to heal the wounds. I stayed all by myself, trying to find a sense to what had happened and wondering how I could have betrayed my family's values to that extent: becoming a woman that obnoxious men such as Leon called whore.

During that period, I was prompted to do some introspection: really, how could anybody, just by looking at me, conclude I was a prostitute? The answer to that was obvious: as my mother once said, there might have been a trashy resonance in the way that I dressed. And, after that, I had taken myself to those risky places. So I had played a huge part in my own misfortune! That revelation greatly distressed me; I only believed I was sexy and admired. That's all I had ever wanted: to be as sexy as I could be. Those thoughts got me so angry that I picked up a pair of scissors, rushed to my closet and cut into pieces all those expensive little dresses that I formerly thought beautiful.

A letter unexpectedly arrived from Courtney. She was thanking me for the time I allowed her to spend in my apartment when she needed a shelter, many months earlier. She wrote that she recognized not having been always agreeable, but that she will treasure our friendship forever. I found this confession rather confusing; my mind wasn't ready to absorb any complicated story. Still I decided, later on, to send her a welcoming card. She had been my friend from childhood, even though our path had kind of shifted now.

One and a half month after the aggression, I was out again, looking for work. It was going to be nothing else but an honest job, this time. I was, at that point, considering going back to New Jersey if there was no opportunity for me around LA. I had planned to arrive to a conclusion in four months. It became also a necessity to subject myself to a few medical tests, in order to detect any potential diseases I could've had contracted following that misadventure.

It was on a Sunday morning, I was watching BET, the Black Entertainment Television, when I heard the song "Change is coming" by Sounds of Blackness. Somehow I was incited to pay attention. Perhaps the rhythm and dynamism of that song had a revitalizing effect on me. I got up and I danced. For the first time since I broke my arm, there was hope in my heart. And I decided, that day, to set aside a little space in my schedule for BET's Sunday celebrations.

And then, Mariam called me. She was in LA and expected that we met. There was a party at Steven's and she insisted that I come. I was about to say no, but I ended thinking « why not? ». Maybe something inside me wanted to revive. And I told her that I'd gladly go to the Steven's party with her.

So it was Steven's anniversary, once again! Was it possible that one year had already passed since the last party? But yeah, one year had passed. Exactly one year ago, I was fostering such great expectations. And here I was today, totally crushed.

Mariam greeted me with her typical smile. She was just superb and I was glad we met again.
— I am delighted to see you again, she murmured when I got into her car.

I was wondering how come she had her own chauffeur in LA since she only comes here once a year. Later on, I would find out that Steven usually made his cars and chauffeurs available for some of his good friends.

Steven's residence now seemed even more impressive than in my memory. Except that I was not as intimidated as the first time I was there. Perhaps, after all that happened to me, I was seeing everything in a different light.

We walked the same paths as a year ago and found ourselves in the same room filled with a vibrant crowd. The music was exhilarating and I unexpectedly sensed some sort of excitement brewing in my body and in my mind. That was to me a forgotten feeling, an energizing impression.

And whatever my troubles might have been, they utterly ceased to exist.

We fought our way to Steven, bearing on our lips a few birthday kisses. There he was, all smiling and looking at us with contentment, as if we were an oasis in the desert. Believe it or not, he had remembered me! Or maybe, he simply concluded that I was the same girl who came with Mariam, the year before. And as I kissed him, he said:
— Here you are again! I am so pleased to see you!

Steven was that kind of person who'd give you his undivided attention; and you would, for a while, believe you were the center of the universe. It was truly a great feeling. Hence I was grateful to be part of his birthday celebration, that night.

After a few drinks at the bar, we jumped on the dance floor. There is no word that could describe the happiness and the craziness that were taking place there. We were under the influence of beats and rhythms; the DJ was terrific and the sound system excellent. Let's just say I was in a state of perfect joy.

I was once reading something about joy. The text explained that joy is one capital virtue; anyone who abides in joy cannot be mischievous. Therefore, joy engenders many good things, as it carries the seeds for favorable relationships, abundance and wholeness. But I was not thinking of that philosophical vision about joy; I was not thinking at all, I was just dancing. And then, right before my eyes, there he was suddenly, in his black turtleneck and his sexy blue jeans: Da-Steel!

I was mesmerized. My heart was pounding and my knees were shaking. At first, I thought I was hallucinating. But rapidly it came to me that Steel had once mentioned seeing me here at the last year party. That little detail had completely slipped away from my mind. Withal, to me, Da-Steel was yet a long gone dream.

Someone said the brain is one great computer. Unless he had said that a computer is like a great brain. Whatever! At that moment, my brain was shifting from all kind of questions and options: was I looking my best? What was I doing one second before he stood in front of me? And how should I behave at this moment? Should I play cold? Should I smile? Was there a chance we became friends again? What should I do now that he was getting closer and closer to me?

But what could I have done? He took me in his arms without saying a single word and we stayed there, huddled up against one another until the song ended. That was when he took my hand and suggested we go outside for a while. And I just followed him without hesitation. There were no more questions in my head; the great computer had logged off.

— What have you been doing since I've last seen you? he asked.
— Let's say I was finding myself.
— Finding yourself! he repeated softly.
He didn't turn his eyes away from me, not for one second.
— You were finding yourself; have you been lost somewhere?
But I was not going to answer that. I could not anyway; I was empty-headed. So I simply smiled.
He shook his head and he murmured:
— I missed you.

There I wasn't smiling anymore. Still, not one word from me. He missed me; would you believe that? I could have questioned him on the reasons why he had not contacted me for so long. Yet, I did keep my mouth shut. The past was past; there was no need trying to bring it back.

— What a magnificent garden!

I intentionally thought out loud, in order to change the subject. And I am sure he understood, because he answered in the strangest way:

— Magnificent it is!

I planted a kiss on his cheek and headed back inside alone. Mariam was at the bar; I decided to ask for another drink. After that, as the DMX's song « *Fame* » got on, we hit the dance floor once again. Except that I was now displaying a fake joy, while inside of me were concocting a lot of confused deliberations. I was anxiously waiting for the moment I'd be alone at home to take stock of that encounter with Da-Steel.

It was past 3 o'clock when Mariam's chauffeur dropped me home. I was tired; however so much was turning over in my mind that I sat down a moment. I started to review all that had occurred during the night, when I heard a knock on my front door. I frankly supposed that Mariam was in need for something and I wasn't too happy about her seeing my apartment's interior and finding out how poor I was. I reluctantly went to the door and opened it. But then, guess who was there in front of me? Da-Steel again!

My heart really escaped a beat. I kind of parted my lips, but yet no word came out. From that very moment I knew that I was lost, that he could do whatever he wanted to do with me. I knew that I was his.

I guess there wasn't much to be said. He took me in his arms and I just closed my eyes. Then the next thing I knew: he was with me in my bed and we were making passionate firing love.

A man's heart will forever remain a mystery to me. Steel came and he was conquered; it was as simple as that. I never understood the reason why; never had the time to question him or myself about that. It all happened as I told you: he did knock at my door one night, and from then on, we were a true couple and we were so in love.

11

It took us only a month to decide to live together. Steel wanted me to move with him from the start. And as soon as my medical test results came all negative, I joined him in his house. Of course, I'd never told him that I had worked as an exotic dancer. He probably could have taken it well enough; nevertheless I thought it'd be a risky move and I kept that misadventure to myself.

Soon after I moved in with Steel, I received the news that Arlene was getting married to her boyfriend Henry. That was good news and I was overjoyed: sincerely, Arlene deserved the best of everything; she was such an amazing woman, generous, loyal and responsible. Henry who had been a sales director in that great company got recently promoted to the position of Sales vice-president. I knew from the start that Henry was the perfect guy for Arlene. And it seemed to me that life was finally taking the right turn.

Living under the same roof had started on a good note for Steel and me: we were in love with each other. Every morning, I would get up and I could not believe I had the chance to be that famous man's girlfriend. And it was so easy living with him, because he was neither arrogant nor vain. It was like being with the guy next door, except that he was filthy rich.

In spite of his popularity, Steel was very receptive to other talented artists in the music industry. I remember how curious he was about the work of hip hop artists outside the States. He was in admiration watching performers like Kardinal Offishall and K-Os, both from Canada.
— This K-Os is an original; he is just fantastic!
And I totally agreed with him on that. I loved the fact that Steel could be humble enough to recognize great talents other than him. That's how he felt about one of his friends, a rapper by the name of Fedeman whom idol was T.I. and who was hoping to become one day a great artist himself.

— It's just a matter of time, my man!
That's what Steel often told Fedeman. And, there was no doubt in my mind, he was totally sincere. He truly believed the guy had star potential.

Living in Steel's house was something I had not anticipated. I believe that when girls talk about becoming a rich man's other half, it is purely theoretical. And if, by chance, such a thing would happen, they would find out that they had never really trusted their desire to come true. As for me, I was living a dream I had not even dared dream of. So, during my first days there, I was in a sort of trance. I was of course taking possession of the multiple rooms and adapting myself to the new lifestyle and neighborhood. But somehow it felt like I was in a temporary situation, some sort of vacation from which I would have soon to return to reality.

And then, there were Steel's wealthy friends. We attended a party on a spectacular private yacht in which were included five bedrooms with their king size bed, many washrooms, a movie theater, a bar, a large living-room and, not to forget, the huge terrace. I later learned that the owner had paid more than two millions for his boat, which he considered a bargain. I happened to fall on another friend's closet that was three times the apartment I used to live in! It is true that Steel had an impressive one too, and you would find in it three hundred pairs of snickers and a hundred designer shoes. I estimated at a quarter Millions of dollars his footwear only. Another successful rapper had paid 200 000$ for just a bottle of Cognac; that was mind-blowing!

It was indeed a whole new existence. We were just taking it easy in our home. We spent most of our time making love, talking about ourselves, laughing, kidding around and doing whatever pleased us. There was music all day long: all kind of music. Steel was really hooked on sounds. I remember we spent a whole day listening and singing to the Outkast's double CD album « *Speakerboxxx / The love below* ». It was a joyful day; we were carried away by such outstanding rhythms. Yeah, it was Big Boi and Andre 3000 at their best. We could understand why so many millions of this album had been sold all over the globe and why it had been so largely rewarded at the 2004 Grammy Awards.

So yes, we sang and we danced all day on Outkast' songs; that was the kind of behavior we indulged in.

Meanwhile, Takisha was a happy wife. Jack had remained a loving husband. She was now pregnant with twins and the couple had plans to move to Atlanta where they had bought a splendid residence.

But for Courtney, things were not going well. That was rather sad; she had such great beginnings. From what I heard afterward, Fern had left her for a new younger girl. He didn't keep his promises, as to help her make a brilliant career; and he didn't care about her future whatsoever. It turned out, since a while ago, that she was working as an escort, because she could not afford her lifestyle anymore: the beautiful apartment, the designer clothes, the drugs. That was a disaster, a true nightmare. Then from most recent news, she too started waiting for clients along the curbs. Yes, that was terribly sad.

Steel got up one day and decided to listen to Rapahel Saadiq's « *Be here* » again and again.

Looking at him singing and simulating playing Saadiq's bass guitar, I felt I was so lucky to have found such a cool and good-looking guy. I ended up laughing because he was also incredibly funny. So I was laughing my head off when he suddenly stopped strumming his imaginary strings, gazed at me and said:

— Baby, let's make a trip to Vegas!

My answer had been a screaming yes; I'd always wanted to go to Las Vegas. So, there we were, wandering along the Strip, feeling like little kids in a giant box of glittering toys, visiting casinos one after another, gaming on slot machines, having quick snacks or eating at buffets, running to attend stunning performances and getting back to our hotel to make love before we go out again. In Las Vegas, for the tourists, there are too many entertainments, not enough time to sleep. We were excited from the moment we got there and long after we left. I was certain that I'd never forget my first trip to Vegas, and indeed I never did.

It was after a Viva Vision Light show at Fremont Street Experience that Steel put one knee on the floor and, in the midst of hundreds of people, said the words.

— You're the woman I love; you are my life. Marry-me, babe!

For a while I thought he was joking; but I quickly understood that was a serious matter. By then, I was astounded. I just took his hand in mine and managed to mutter an inaudible « yes, I will ». Next thing I knew, Steel sprung up and announced with a surprising enthusiasm:

— Aright baby, let's go!

And from that moment, everything went very fast.

It was once a Wedding Chapel in Las Vegas. We were there, among a few others, waiting to get married. And came our turn: Steel and I became man and wife. That's it that's all.

Right after the ceremony, we landed on the Strip again. I was walking on air. The man I was in love with had just committed himself to me in an extreme fashion. I could not process what had happened. Yet my heart was filled with passion and gratitude. I stood still for a moment; I needed to take a good look at my husband. Steel was smiling at me and there could be no doubt: he loved me. He took me in his arms and solemnly declared:

— Jenny, you are my wife now. You are my queen; I adore you.

We got back home and easily picked up where we left off. But it was a new kind of energy. We could not be happier; we were confident that our love would last forever and that we'd be together until the end of time.

It was important to me to have a traditional marriage ceremony. My mother would certainly not comprehend that we were really married otherwise. I guess I also wanted to fulfill an every woman's dream: a real wedding with the sumptuous white dress, the veil, the reception, in the presence of everyone I knew. And, of course, Steel was to provide the big diamond ring.

My mother, Arlene and Henry, Takisha and Jack; they all were coming. I had invited Courtney and a few LA acquaintances as well. During that time of my life, I only had love in my heart: pure love.

And I was so certain that loving state of mind would reside in me forever.

We had rented a banqueting hall in a well-known hotel. The decorations and the catering were included in the lease. All we had to do was to bring ourselves and the guests. It was a very elegant crowd. Mariam had made the trip to LA again; she would not have missed my wedding for the world! I just could not believe she would have traveled from London for a one day function. But that's how Mariam was.

The ceremony was unfolding superbly. The place was outstanding and the food exquisite. Everyone had complimented me on my look and had wished Steel and me a happy life together. There was a mountain of gifts at one of the corners of the hall. It was just marvelous.

Joanna, an ex-colleague dancer, came to offer her greetings. And while Steel was pulled away by another group of our friends, she expressed to me her joy for the occurrence of our marriage.
— Jenny, I wish you a wonderful conjugal life. May God bless your union with an endless joy!

— Oh thank you so much, Joanna!

— I recall what Nora has done to you when she realized that Da-Steel was interested in you!

— Nora?... Really? What has she done?

By then, I already knew what Joanna was about to say. I could remember that day: Nora was coming close to me a few seconds before I fell and broke my arm.

— I saw her, Jenny…

— Please Joanna, please go on!

— You were to perform a very difficult step and she kicked your heel while she was dancing.

— You mean she did it on purpose?

— Yes, of course she did; and I was the only one who saw her doing it.

After Joanna explained to me that Nora had intentionally caused me to fall during that video shooting, I was really disturbed. There is always something distressful in acknowledging that people would deliberately hurt you for no reason. Well, Nora had been jealous of me; but obviously I was not responsible for Da-Steel liking me. And how come Joanna had kept that story secret for such a long time? These thoughts were invading my mind, and my wedding day was becoming all gloomy. However, I exhorted myself to remain positive; I was not going to let Nora's wickedness spoil our beautiful moment. For such a good thing had resulted from that fall: I married Steel.

My good mood was fully recovered when Courtney came up to me. She took my face in her hand, looked at me a moment and she smiled. She then kissed me on both cheeks. I was now really proud that I invited her because it seemed so clear to me that she had remained my best friend after all. That is when she murmured in my ear:

— I envy you; he's such a good fucker!

— What!?

— Yes, believe me, he is.

— And how would you happen to know that?

— Well, come on, Jenny, he fucked me a few times. He really did. He did fuck me so hard; that was better than ecstasy!

— Really!? And when was that?

— Almost two years ago, you know.

I was trying to keep my cool, but I could feel my whole body trembling as a brutal turmoil was

138

erupting in me. Miraculously, I managed to appear calm and collected when I asked her:

— Almost two years ago? You mean when you were living in my apartment?

— But yes, Jenny.

— And you never told me.

— That had nothing to do with you, right?

— Yeah, you're right.

Once again, I was about to surprise myself: I put my hand on her shoulder and smiled broadly. Then I kissed her on both cheeks too. I guess I could call that a conscious act of hypocrisy, but a genuine goodbye kiss. To me, Courtney no longer existed.

I was still smiling when I walked toward my husband and took him in my arms. Still smiling while we danced on Shania Twain's « *From this moment on* » and when we kissed in front of the people applauding. I was smiling when I gazed at him, and I am sure what he saw in my eyes was ardent love. Thanks God, there was no way he could have read inside my mind, where was brewing my bitterness. Thanks God he could not see that under the pristine white dress, a dark and

139

angry heart was pounding fiercely. Yeah, I was still smiling: the show had to go on. That's it that's all.

A RAPPER'$ QUEEN – PART II

by MMANDI

IS COMING SOON

PUBLISHING, MISE EN PAGE AND ILLUSTRATION
QUART-DE-LUNE ÉDITIONS & LOISIRS INC.